Acknowledgements

I would like to thank my Year 5 students who helped me to finalise my ideas. Especially Alfie and Aubrey whose verses are included in my book (lightsaber and boxing verses). I'd like to thank my friends and family who helped me to edit, improve and format my story. Also, I'd like to thank my talented illustrator who brought my story to life with his wonderful drawings.

In your town lives a
super magical baby,

But I don’t think anyone knows,

Does she hide the powers in her
fingers?

Or in a secret cape under her clothes?

She wakes up her parents early for work,

Like an army soldier, sharp and alert.

And what do you know? She's a great artist too,

Painting the walls and dad's odd shoe.

She's a great doctor and saves patients,

Using herbal recipes that are very ancient.

he can take to the skies, way up past the trees,

In her suit and her cape, as super as can be.

In your town lives a super magical baby,

But I don't think anyone knows,

Does she hide the powers in her fingers?

Or in a secret cape under her clothes?

She can climb across the monkey bars,

Reaching high up into the stars.

She steers her own pushchair,

Racing faster than her neighbour Claire.

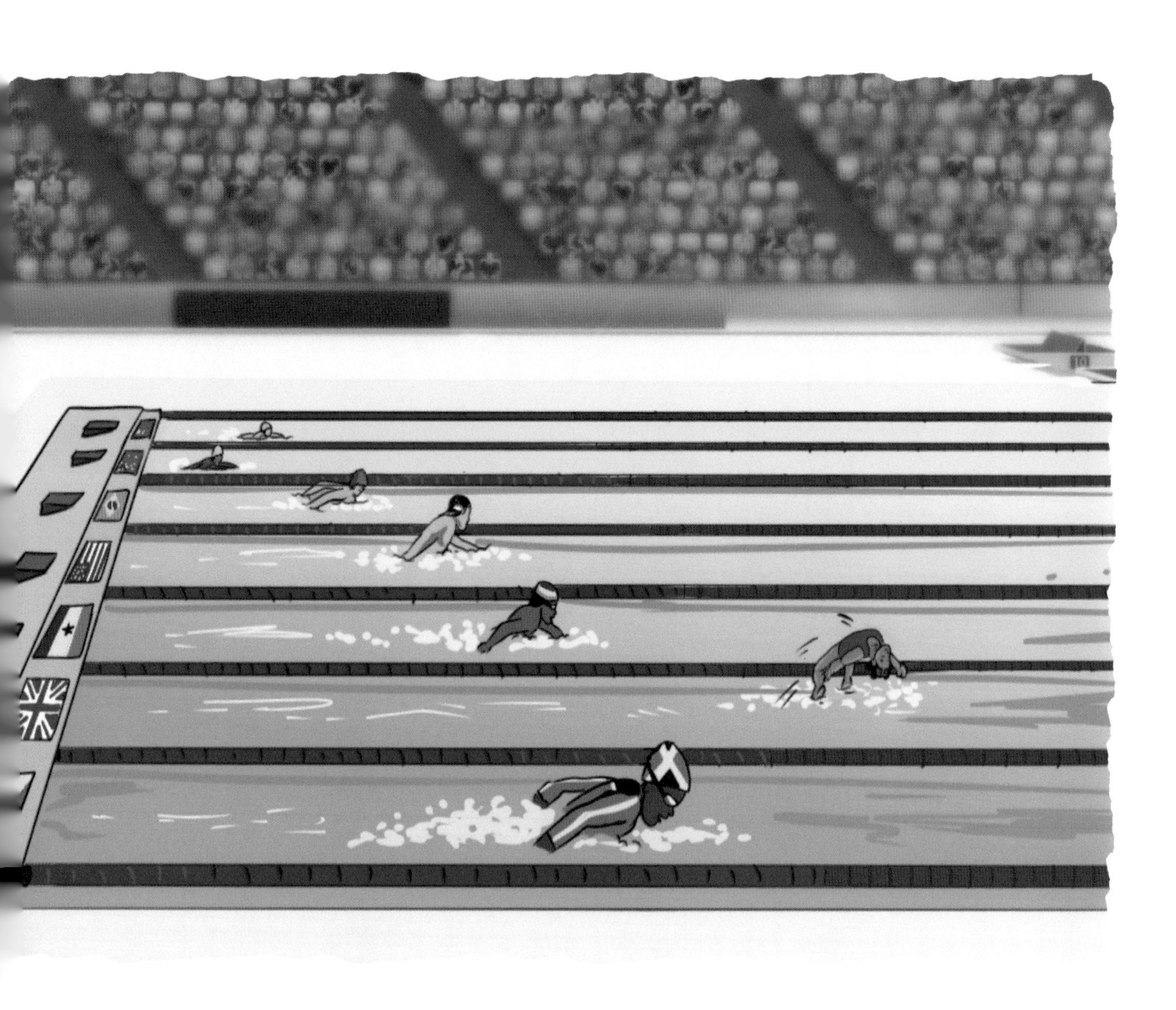

In water she's like a swimmer at the Olympics,

Doing tricks like dives and backflips.

And another thing is, she's a great musician,

Making up her own compositions.

In your town lives a super magical baby,

But I don’t think anyone knows,

Does she hide the powers in her fingers?

Or in a secret cape under her clothes?

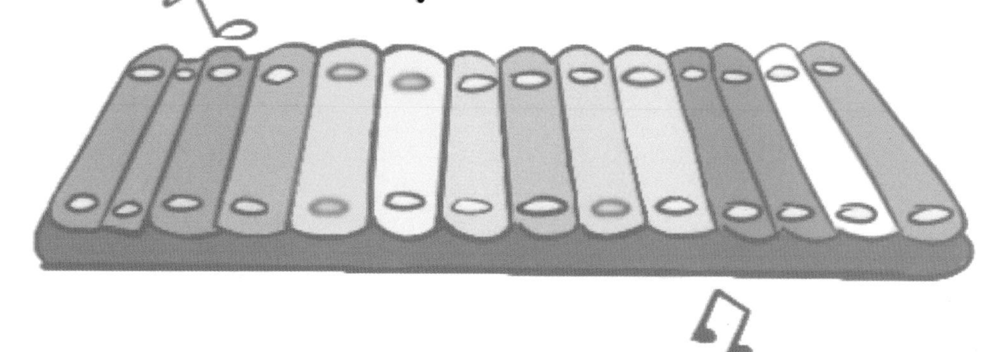

She protects others from naughty toddlers,

Like the mischievous, cheeky Teddy Cobbler.

The angry boy once tried to bite,

So they got into a lightsaber fight!

SUN
MERCURY
VENUS
EARTH
ASTEROIDS
COMETS

She learnt to ride on her two-wheeler,

Without anyone having to teach her.

She flies around in a private jet,

Covering distant lands like Peru and Tibet.

And when she's in her super-suit,

She makes light work of her veg and fruit.

In your town lives a super magical baby,

But I don't think anyone knows,

Does she hide the powers in her fingers?

Or in a secret cape under her clothes?

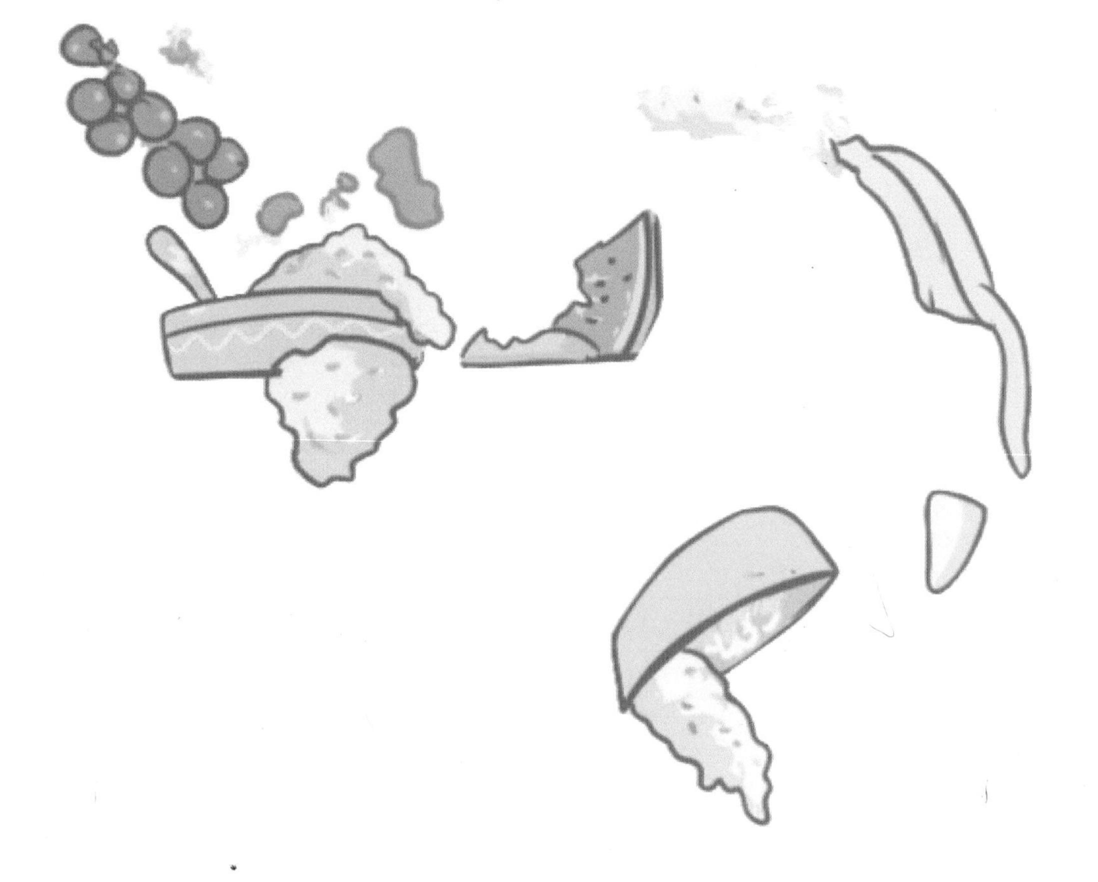

She's got the knack for horse riding,

And flashes past everyone like lightening.

She can push herself high up on the swings,

It's as if she was born with wings.

You might not think, but she's a great cook,

And she has a super recipe book.

She is strong and can win anything,

Knocking out boxers in the ring!

ould you be your
wn's next magical hero?

ou can do amazing things too
you have a go,

's good fun like a celebration,

ll you have to do is use your
nagination.

The End

What's your super magical name?

Printed in Great Britain
by Amazon